EARLY BIRD
STORIES™

Doctors
in My Community

Bridget Heos   Illustrated by **Mike Moran**

LERNER PUBLICATIONS ◆ MINNEAPOLIS

NOTE TO EDUCATORS

Find text recall questions at the end of each chapter. Critical-thinking and text feature questions are available on page 23. These help young readers learn to think critically about the topic by using the text, text features, and illustrations.

Lerner Publications Company
A division of Lerner Publishing Group, Inc.
241 First Avenue North
Minneapolis, MN 55401 USA

For reading levels and more information, look up this title at www.lernerbooks.com.

Photos on page 22 used with permission of: Stuart Jenner/Shutterstock.com (doctors); omphoto/Shutterstock.com (medical supplies); Blackroom/Shutterstock.com (stethoscope).

Main body text set in Billy Infant 22/28.
Typeface provided by SparkyType.

Library of Congress Cataloging-in-Publication Data

Names: Heos, Bridget, author. | Moran, Michael, 1957- illustrator.
Title: Doctors in my community / Bridget Heos ; illustrated by Mike Moran.
Description: Minneapolis : Lerner Publications, [2018] | Series: Meet a community helper (Early bird stories) | Audience: Ages 5–8. | Audience: K to grade 3. | Includes bibliographical references and index.
Identifiers: LCCN 2017060516 (print) | LCCN 2017049363 (ebook) | ISBN 9781541524118 (eb pdf) | ISBN 9781541520233 (lb : alk. paper) | ISBN 9781541527065 (pb : alk. paper)
Subjects: LCSH: Pediatricians—Juvenile literature. | Physicians—Juvenile literature.
Classification: LCC RJ78 (print) | LCC RJ78 .H455 2018 (ebook) | DDC 610.69/5—dc23

LC record available at https://lccn.loc.gov/2017060516

Manufactured in the United States of America
1-44359-34605-3/22/2018

TABLE OF CONTENTS

CHAPTER 1

THE YOUNGEST PATIENTS

Our class wants to learn what doctors do!

Dr. Zambil is a pediatrician.
That's a doctor who treats children.

Dr. Zambil works in a clinic.

His patients are babies, children, and teenagers.

"I find out what's wrong," he says.

"They may need medicine or rest. Sometimes they need to go to the hospital."

J.J. says, "I went to the hospital when I was little. But I'm better now."

"That's our goal!" Dr. Zambil says. "We want you to be healthy so you can reach your goals too."

What is the name for a doctor who treats children?

CHAPTER 2

CHECKUPS

"I went to the doctor when I wasn't sick," Katya says.

"That's good," Dr. Zambil says. "Kids should get a checkup once a year."

HEALTHY FOOD

He checks their ears. He listens to their hearts. He asks if they eat healthy food. These things help kids stay well.

"Do you give kids shots?" Paul asks.

"Yes," Dr. Zambil says. "So do nurses. They know how to make the shots hurt less."

What do doctors do at a checkup?

CHAPTER 3

DOCTOR SCHOOL

We learn that Dr. Zambil went to college for four years. Then he had medical school and training for seven years.

That's a *lot* of homework!

"When I'm not at the clinic, I teach at the hospital," Dr. Zambil says.

"My students learn to be doctors by seeing real patients."

Lainey raises her hand. "I was a real patient. I went to the hospital when I broke my arm."

"You probably had an X-ray." Dr. Zambil holds one up.

"X-rays are pictures that show the bones and organs inside your body."

Thanks, Dr. Zambil, for helping us
stay healthy!

For how many years do doctors go to medical school and training?

LEARN ABOUT COMMUNITY HELPERS

Doctors are workers in the community. A community is a group of people who live or work in the same city, town, or neighborhood.

Sick or injured children may see a specialist. A specialist is a doctor who treats one part of the body, such as the heart. Some specialists are also pediatricians.

Doctors check ears with a tool called an otoscope. They listen to the heart with a stethoscope.

Doctors write prescriptions for medicine. A prescription tells what medicine a patient needs. It also tells the patient when to take the medicine.

Shots make you immune to some diseases, such as measles. That means your body protects itself from the germs that cause the disease.

THINK ABOUT COMMUNITY HELPERS:
CRITICAL-THINKING AND TEXT FEATURE QUESTIONS

Why do you think doctors go through so much schooling?

Why is it important for medical school students to practice on real patients before they become doctors?

Where can you find the table of contents of this book?

What do the chapter titles of this book tell you about each chapter's main idea?

GLOSSARY

medicine: substances swallowed or put on the skin to treat an illness or injury

nurse: a person who is trained to care for the sick or injured and to help others stay healthy

patient: a person who receives medical care

X-ray: a picture that shows teeth, bones, and organs inside the body

TO LEARN MORE

BOOKS

Kenan, Tessa. *Hooray for Doctors!* Minneapolis: Lerner Publications, 2018. Read this book to learn more about how doctors help us stay healthy.

Morris, J. E. *Fish Are Not Afraid of Doctors.* New York: Penguin Workshop, 2018. In this story, Maud is nervous about visiting the doctor, but soon she learns a checkup isn't so bad!

WEBSITE

Going to the Doctor
http://kidshealth.org/en/kids/going-to-dr.html#
Find out what to expect during a visit to the doctor, and learn what different parts of a checkup tell the doctor about your health.

INDEX